MONSTROUS MORALS

Also In The Series

Nose–Picker Nick is the story of what happens to a boy who can't stop picking his nose. He ends up going inside his own nose and having a terrifying confrontation with The Bogeyman.

Grubby Joe Grub tells of the boy who refused to get washed. He turns into a dirty pig and is taken off to the abattoir, only to be saved in the nick of time.

Scary Hairy Mary is a warning to everyone who doesn't brush their hair, as Mary gets lost in a terrifying jungle.

Black–toothed Ruth Black never brushes her teeth – and gets carried away by the evil Tooth Devils.

Excessively Messy Bessie is one of those children who won't keep their bedrooms tidy – and finds herself in the biggest mess of her life at Devil's Dump.

Chilly Billy Winters is a boy who refuses to wrap up warm – and gets kidnapped by a gang of zombie snowmen.

Gobby Nobby Robinson is a boy who can't stop talking – and is caught in a terrifying mouth-trap.

Smelly Simon Smedley never changes his socks – so Bigfoot pays a visit.

ISBN 978-1-908211-09-5

A catalogue record for this book is available from the British Library.

First published in Great Britain in 2012 by Pro-actif Communications
Cameron House, 42 Swinburne Road, Darlington, Co Durham DL3 7TD
email: books@carpetbombingculture.co.uk
© Pro-actif Communications

Peter Barron

www.monstrousmorals.co.uk

A warning to children who are full of hot air - stop breaking wind or you'd better beware!

PLEASE NOTE THAT THIS BOOK IS NOT FOR PARENTS OF A DELICATE DISPOSITION. CONSIDER YOURSELF DULY CAUTIONED...

THERE was no one who ever embarrassed you more,
Than Martin Sidebottom, the kid from next door.
Martin was one of those horrible boys,
Who was expert at making a rude kind of noise...

At the back of the classroom
he sat there and grinned,
As he leaned to one side, held
his breath and broke wind.
Blaming his friends for the
smell which was rotten,
As he parted his cheeks and
let rip with his bottom.

His mum was aghast
at such sounds from
her son,
But to Martin a gust
just meant having fun.
He'd lost count of the
folk he had deeply
offended,
Taking the view that's
what nature intended.

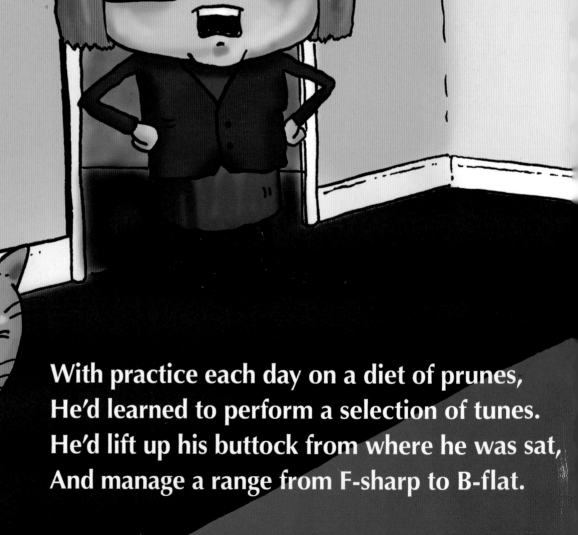

With practice each day on a diet of prunes,
He'd learned to perform a selection of tunes.
He'd lift up his buttock from where he was sat,
And manage a range from F-sharp to B-flat.

With that kind of skill, he was soon in demand,
To play in a show with the village brass band.

Alf Watts, the conductor, was short of a trumpet,
But Mart had an instrument known as a 'pump-it'.

Fartin' Martin was startin' to get rave reviews,
The boy with the musical bottom was news.
A piece in the paper was glowing, I quote:
"Sidebottom's a star – not a single bum note."

The band's reputation spread from nation to nation,
Every full house gave a standing ovation.
They performed round the world but the highlight of all,
Was a request to play at the Royal Albert Hall.

Young Martin was poised to fulfil his dream:
To play a wind solo in front of The Queen.
But depressing dark clouds hung over London that night,
And the band could sense something wasn't quite right.

As soon as Alf Watts had raised up his baton,
A breeze stirred beneath the chair Mart was sat on.
With each wave of Alf's stick, the wind gathered pace,
And the look of the devil spread over his face.

This wasn't the Alf the band had expected,
A kindly old man so widely respected.
This was a beast who'd grown horns and a tail,
While conjuring up the most violent gale.

By now Alf was red, the colour of blood,
He was flailing his arms as fast as he could.
The band couldn't stop, playing faster and faster,
And Martin could sense an impending disaster.

The hall was in chaos, children were crying,
People took cover as chairs were sent flying.
The Queen was the first to be rescued, of course,
For the breeze was now blowing at hurricane force.

The band took the full blast of the devilish wind,
It ripped off their clothes, then peeled off their skins.
A skeleton crew with xylophone bones,
Were left playing the trumpets, horns and trombones.

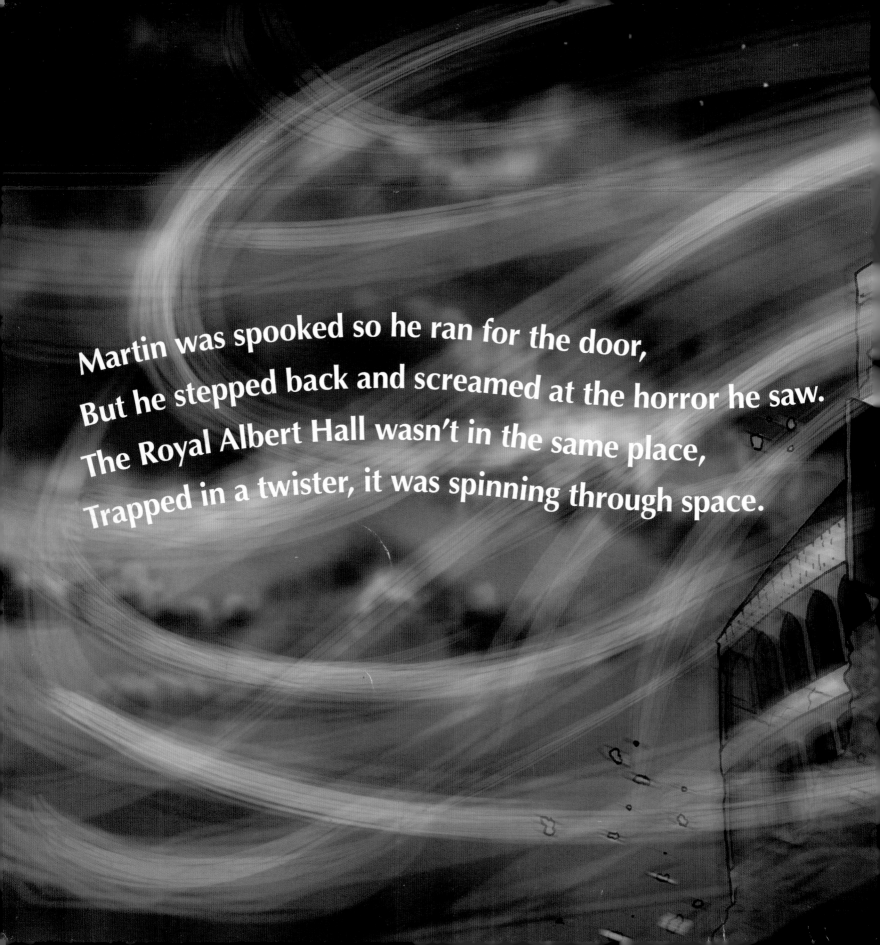

Martin was spooked so he ran for the door,
But he stepped back and screamed at the horror he saw.
The Royal Albert Hall wasn't in the same place,
Trapped in a twister, it was spinning through space.

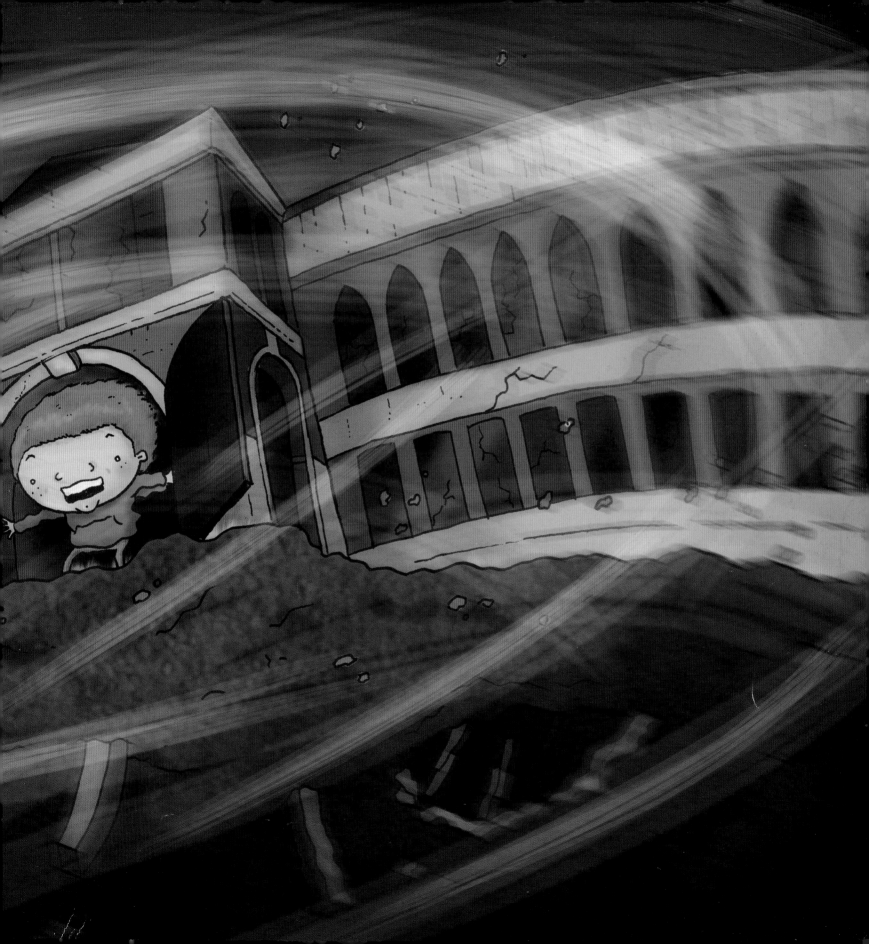

Martin's worst nightmare now seemed complete,
As he zoomed over the earth at 3,000 feet.
His nerves were so bad that his wind was quite chronic,
As the hall reached a speed that topped supersonic.

In the eye of the storm, the worst ever seen,
He blew for his life, playing God Save The Queen.
But Her Highness was gone – she was now safe and sound,
In a nuclear bunker, deep underground.

The Royal Albert Hall with turbulence tumbled,
As Martin's poor tummy with flatulence grumbled.
In the clouds he could hear the blood–curdling screeches,
Of the vilest, the smelliest, the ugliest creatures.

Over the years, he'd been in quite a few scrapes,
But he was under attack from a squadron of apes.
One–eyed gorillas and long-haired baboons,
Were bombarding the hall from hot-air balloons.

One minute the sky could not
have been duller,
The next it was vivid –
a riot of colour.
Purple ones, orange ones,
blue ones and pink ones,
Deadly balloons dropping
jet–propelled stink bombs.

The skeleton band played on
through the gloom,
But Martin just spluttered,
choking on fumes.
He held on to his breath for all
he was worth,
This was air straight from hell –
the bowels of the earth.

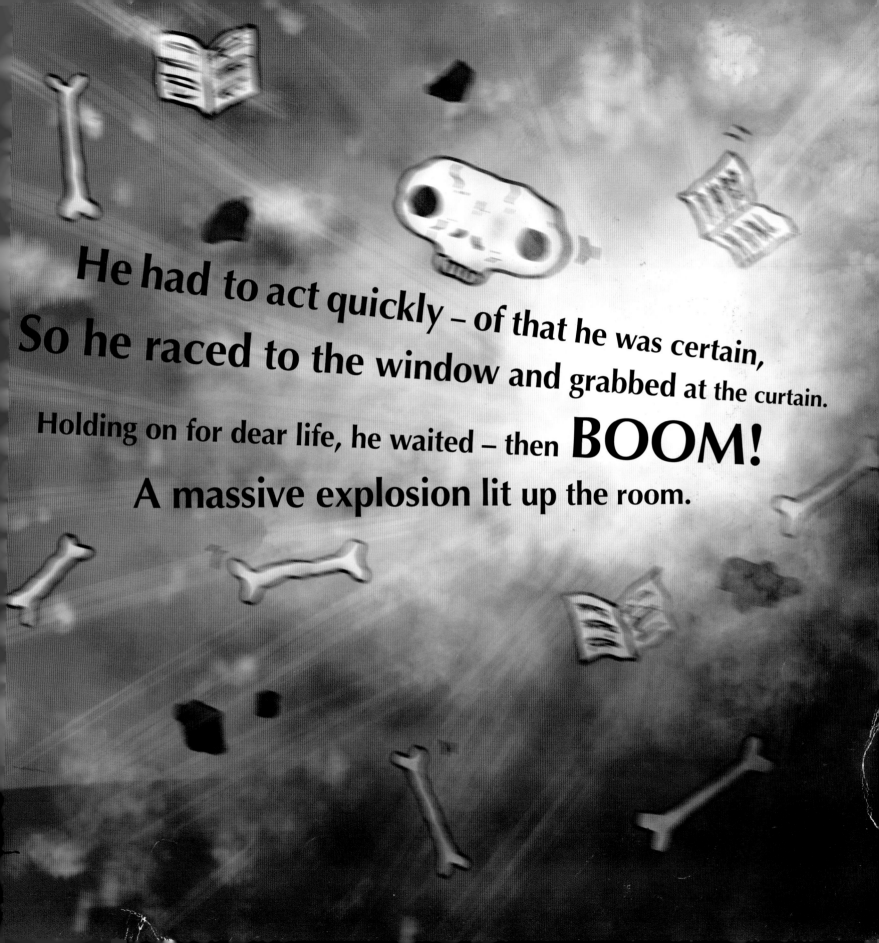

He had to act quickly – of that he was certain,
So he raced to the window and grabbed at the curtain.

Holding on for dear life, he waited – then **BOOM!**

A massive explosion lit up the room.

The Royal Albert Hall was blown into bits,
And Mart was left plunging, scared out of his wits.
But just as he'd hoped, the drapes from the hall,
Began putting the brakes on the speed of his fall.

In the midst of it all, Mart had been rather cute,

He'd dodged death by creating his own parachute.

Floating through clouds without further assistance,

He spotted his home away in the distance.

He was missing his mum so that's where he went,

Adjusting the cords to control his descent.

And when the wind dropped, Martin wasn't too fussed,

He just flexed his bottom to provide extra thrust.

When he came in to land in his mother's back garden,
Martin uttered a word he'd not used before – "Pardon".
His ordeal had taught him what's wrong and what's right:
If you happen to fart, you must please be polite.

Now, his trousers are silent, he smells like a rose,
A boy most unlikely to get up your nose.
He's not knowingly rude – in fact to be fair,
Martin Sidebottom's a real breath of fresh air.

And the monstrous moral of this story...
If you can't control your bottom, an ill–wind will be blowing!